small things matter

(happiness depends on them)

R.Kesavamurthi

aelay
publish

small things matter (happiness depends on them)
Poetry

by R.Kesavamurthi 2022 ©
First Edition : November 2022
Pages: 53
ISBN : 978-93-5533-608-8
Aelay Publish
Contact : +91 9944992571
Designed by : Aelay publish team

CONTENTS

S.NO.	TOPIC	POEMS
1	EDUCATION, KNOWLEDGE	01 - 20
2	LIFE, PARENTING	21 - 42
3	BUSINESS, TECHNOLOGY	43 - 51
4	PERSONALITY	52 - 72
5	SOCIAL ISSUES	73 - 86
6	NATURE, HEALTH	87-100

EDUCATION, KNOWLEDGE

Learn from unconventional sources!

Cooking from male chefs! Negotiation from mothers!

Technology from youth! Subjects from co-students!

With some changes, a little effort,

One can impress with speaking skills!

People judge based on spoken command!

Learn from a competent teacher

Reflect on it until doubts are resolved

Ponder and absorb completely

No study is a waste

Of those interested a few are committed

Fewer pursue until it is assimilated

Knowledge is gained by devoting attention

Information and knowledge are two different things

Google provides just information

Comprehend the concept beyond understanding

Ask what if formula (eg: F=ma) is not true

Ensure success in JEE / NEET Type Exams

Competitive exams are tough

Learn concepts, write tests, find gaps

Scoring becomes easier

Education system is in crossroads

Skills, ethics and values are in deficit

Knowledge is in surplus

Engineers are backbone of India

Food delivery to Programming is Engineers' Forte!!

An All-Purpose Graduate (APG)?

World class education

Cutting edge ideas

Practical solutions to human challenges

Knowledge is power

Skill is practical and important

Good values are more important

Ignorance breeds fear

Knowledge removes fear

Fear goes away with direct confrontation

Game knowledge and presentation is art

Knowledge is science and presentation art

Fusion art and science for success

What matters in school education?

Teachers and teaching matter most,

Boards does not matter much.

Repetition leads to perfection

Incremental improvement is the key

Frequent improvements are mandatory

Disciple and Student ask questions

student questions the answer

Disciple trusts and accepts the answer

Anxious to do well in exams?

Nervousness in doing?

Impacts the performance

Get quality education at affordable cost!

Identify premier institutes in your study area!

Commit yourself to join there!

Reading is a good habit!

Notes-making must follow reading!

Learn to communicate by reading!

Education and ethics are complementary!

Those are essentials to enjoy life!

Both help to choose moral ways!

LIFE

Reasoning is guiding star of life

Challenge the existing beliefs in all aspects

Don't fall prey for blind faith

Integrity in life

Commitment beyond self interest

Inspires others

Small things matter

Happiness depends on them

Pay attention

Learn something new always

Build ideas with positive attitude

Secrets of feeling young

Life and economy are complex like biology

Humans try to fit mathematical models

End up with only partial solutions

The more we learn

More things we find there is to learn

Ignorance grows exponentially with knowledge

Who am I?

Identification with Body, Mind or Intellect

Is the reflection of ego

All life struggles are 2 categories

Trying to get something

Trying to get rid of something

Not drag past into present

Not live in dreams

Live in the present, where past meets future

Suicide attempt is an egoistic act

Feelings of my wish/goals are too strong

Perish the ego and immerse in life

Some have problem of excess

Others have problem of scarcity

Out-of-box solutions is need of the hour

Children need no correction

Every child is normal and unique

They need just inspiration

Do what matters to you

Do what is needed for the situation

Enjoy a blissful life journey

Basic defect of parents

They desire worldly success for their children

Children sacrifice their happiness

Pay intense attention to kids

It throws open many doors for them

Kids potential is unleashed

Young mothers can work from home

They can become near full-time mom

Good for the new born

Loosen purse for education and food

Tighten it for jewels, dresses and vehicles

Strike a situation specific balance

Happiness is found within

Extended period of happiness helps

Reach full potential by stretching limits

Each child is unique

Appreciate uniqueness to realise individuality

Embracing individuality builds self esteem

Prepare the child for situations,

Equip them to understand environment,

Besides passing on survival tricks

Consciousness must mould human lives

Best life can be built on creative impulses

Liberation of creativeness is principle of life

Longing to win becomes obstacle in winning!

Longing for power becomes obstacle in getting power!

Longing to live eternally becomes obstacle in living!

BUSINESS

Business needs to make money

Unit economics is mandatory for start-ups

Scaling up ensures growth

Quality control is a post-mortem!

Quality assurance is a preventive action!

Quality is in the minds of people!

Purpose leads to goals

Clarity of goals is a way to succeed

Confidence without clarity is a disaster

Projects are broken up into parts

Skilled persons deal part suited them

Team work brings success and efficiency

 small things matter

Gig economy suits all?

Youngsters, females and retirees!

Marriage of job and convenience!

Computers and handphones are wonder machines

Capacity of society unleashed

Conscious and judicious use is mandatory

Technology provides energy efficient gadgets

Conservation of nature is the present-day need

Being frugal is nature

Example of out-of-box thinking!

Select young barbers worked during pandemic!

Shared income with the whole community!

Close observation of achievers reveal,

Success is outcome of working joyfully,

Luck is an outcome of hard work!

PERSONALITY

Outspokenness is not appreciated largely

Headache is common excuse to avoid embarrassment

Useful blessing to mankind

Perception influences decisions

It reflects reality but not always

Quality at affordable price wins

Devil dares

Dare devil is not scared

Success follows the later

Do you read voraciously?

Can write 80% economics books from memory

Reply of Ex CM Annadurai

Etiquette gives self confidence

The way we behave, talk, walk

Behaving same with rich and poor

Be polite to everyone

Don't let subordinates take you for granted

Treat them with respect

What made Gandhi a Mahatma

Stood in defence of truth

Remarkable quality is courage of the soul

Hitler is a teetotaller

Kindness and good habits need not co-exist

He killed 6 million in wars

Confidence brings better focus on goals

Capacities are a state of mind

Be an optimist

Term "hardwork" is often misunderstood

**Attentiveness with knowledge and skill
are prerequisites**

Hardwork never fails

Involvement leads to success

Intense attentiveness brings involvement

It opens up hidden things

Humans learn through perceptions

Acquire capabilities through knowledge and experience

Learn to find inborn capabilities

Senses grasp attributes of objects

Perception projects an image by integrating attributes

Memory is storage space of images

Don't fall prey for blind faith

Challenge the existing beliefs in all respects

Reasoning is guiding star of life

Never exaggerate success or failure

Never underestimate possibility and reality

Never ever give up

Intense attentiveness brings involvement!

Involvement opens up hidden talents!

Talent leads to new possibilities!

Smile has power

Smiling indicates happiness and friendliness

Communication is better with smile

Good deeds are important

Compulsive nature is like a knife

Compulsiveness even for doing good is bad

Align career with strengths and opportunities

Use time and money in upgradation

Believe yourself and ensure grand success

Fear is natural and common too

Fear of failure can make us inactive

Deal with root cause to overcome fear

Punctuality adds value to life

A must to achieve success in life

Time and tide wait for none

SOCIAL ISSUES

Two parallel lines signify an equal sign

Symbolic language of equality

Relation of two entities that appear different

Good and bad are geographical

Tibetan custom allows many husbands

Monogamy is virtue in India

Associate with good people

Know what is possible in life

Aspire and get there

Best decisions evolve from roots

Understand role of the most unimportant person

To attain VIP category

Man talks an experience without living it

Can discuss hunger when well fed

This distinguishes man from animals

Bring better understanding of other sex

Reduce sexual harassment incidences

Coeducation schooling may help

Tolerance is accepting others as they are

It works even where love fails

Tolerance is most needed now

Dog chases and cat runs

Dog doesn't know what to do if he catches her

Man is not so kind as dogs

Corporate Social Responsibility (CSR) is mandatory

Individual Social Responsibility (ISR) is voluntary

Both CSR and ISR are obligatory

Change is the only constant

Resource scarcity, rigidity, owning mindset was the past

Flexibility, Sharing are the present

Shopping is an entertainment

Need not spend too much time

Should not buy unwanted things

New year marks new beginning

Hope for good times

Hope for new opportunities

Infrastructure infringes nature

Climate change triggers disasters

Humans try sustainable infrastructure

Liberty is not a personal affair

It is an accommodation of interests

Liberty is a social contract

HEALTH & NATURE

Good health is the best

Right medics at right time is better

Confidence on treatment is prerequisite

Health is true wealth

Compulsiveness is cause for modern diseases

Consciousness brings well being

Consuming less energy for given task

Irrigating more land with available water

Being frugal is nature

When being closer to nature

Decisions made are good

Nature is the most reliable energiser

To err is human

Not to err is super human

To forgive is divine

Students are backbone of India

Physical education provides fitness

Fit Indians make demographic dividend a reality

Birth and death happen everyday

Yet people act as if life is permanent

This is the greatest wonder in the world

Many discoveries are accidental

Columbus unexpectedly found western hemisphere

Discoveries come unsought

Science does not rely on beliefs!

It deals with verifiable facts!

Reasoning with experiments reveal facts!

Important foods for healthy life

Onion pures blood; Carrot boosts immunity.

Tomato protects skin; Greens good for eyes.

Eating Tomatoes Daily

Keeps

Cancer and Heart Failure Away!

Water is a unique liquid!

It maintains life on earth!

Its flow makes or breaks agriculture!

Postural habit affects our thoughts!

Nutrition influences our moods!

Body condition impacts our feelings!

Physical education keeps children fit!

It improves mind and body!

It must be taught in schools!